LETTERS HOME
from
JAPAN

Marcia S. Gresko

BLACKBIRCH PRESS, INC.
WOODBRIDGE, CONNECTICUT

Published by Blackbirch Press, Inc.
260 Amity Road
Woodbridge, CT 06525

©2000 by Blackbirch Press, Inc.
First Edition

e-mail: staff@blackbirch.com
Web site: www.blackbirch.com

Printed in Singapore

10 9 8 7 6 5 4 3 2 1

All photographs ©Corel Corporation

Library of Congress Cataloging-in-Publication Data
Gresko, Marcia S.
Letters home from—Japan / by Marcia S. Gresko.
    p.   cm.
Includes bibliographical references and index.
Summary: Describes some of the sights and experiences on a trip through Japan, including
visits to Tokyo, Mount Fuji, Nara, Kumamoto, and Hiroshima.
ISBN 1-56711-409-1
1. Japan—Description and travel.—Juvenile literature.
 I. Title: Japan. II. Title.
DS812.G74 2000
915.204'40—dc21   99-045467

TABLE OF CONTENTS

Arrival in . . .

Tokyo

Yesterday we arrived in Tokyo, the capital city of Japan. Tokyo is located on the island of Honshu. That's the largest of Japan's four main islands.

Check out the map, and you'll see that Japan is really a group of islands just east of mainland Asia. This kind of close grouping of islands is called an archipelago. Japan's 4 main islands—and more than 4,000 others—stretch for about 1,700 miles. Altogether, they make up a country about the size of California. According to legend, the islands were formed from drops of water falling from a god's jeweled sword.

Our tour guide refers to Japan as Nippon, or Nihon, which means "source of the sun."

CHINA

RUSSIA

NORTH KOREA

Sapporo

Hokkaido

Sea of Japan

Akita

SOUTH KOREA

Honshu

JAPAN

North Pacific Ocean

Takayama

Nagano
Tokyo

Kofu

Hiroshima

Kyoto

Kamakura

Miyajima

Nara

Osaka

Kumamoto

Shikoku

Kyushu

East China Sea

I'm here!

Tokyo

Wow, Tokyo is crowded! Our guide said it's one of the world's most populated cities. Over 75% of Japan's 126 million people are packed into cities located on flat coastal plains. Tokyo's more than 8 million people live in tiny apartments in high-rise buildings, or in small, wooden houses.

No matter what time of day it is in Tokyo, it's rush hour! Huge traffic jams constantly halt the rush of cars, cabs, trucks, and buses. Workers on motorcycles and bikes squeeze through the crush. Tokyo is Japan's transportation center. "Bullet trains" travel at 150 miles per hour between major cities.

Bullet trains, Tokyo Station

Rush hour in Tokyo

Tokyo
telephones

Pedestrian
crossing

Some people in the train seemed curious about us. Very few non-Japanese people live in Japan. For thousands of years its island location kept foreigners away. In more recent times, Japanese leaders wouldn't allow outsiders to enter. The country has only been open to visitors for about 130 years!

Tokyo

We began our tour today at the Tokyo Tower. Modeled after the Eiffel Tower in Paris, it's one of the tallest human-made structures on Earth. From the observation deck, Tokyo looks like a forest of glass and steel skyscrapers!

Our next stop was the Ginza District. This is the city's most elegant shopping section. Stores here sell everything from fashionable clothing and glowing pearl jewelry to hi-tech electronic equipment and motorcycles.

Ginza District

Tokyo Tower

Cherry blossoms
in Shinjuku park

Tokyo is Japan's commercial, financial, and industrial center. International corporations are headquartered here, and the Tokyo Stock Exchange is one of the world's largest. Huge factories produce electronic goods, such as computers, cameras, and VCRs. Others produce chemicals, food, furniture, and paper products.

But Tokyo is not all business! After work, businesspeople often relax in pachinko (pinball) parlors and karaoke bars. On the weekends, people enjoy the city's restaurants and sights. There are ancient shrines and temples, fine museums, and peaceful gardens. Baseball games and sumo wrestling matches are also popular. There's even a Disneyland here!

Tokyo

I can see why Tokyo is the center for Japan's performing arts. There's so much to do! Last night's performance of a kabuki play at the National Theater was awesome! Kabuki is Japan's best-known kind of theater. The plays tell stories from Japanese history, legends, and folktales. I was surprised to learn that all the heavily made-up performers were male!

Musical groups present concerts of traditional Japanese music, featuring such Japanese instruments as the three-stringed shamisen and the koto, a kind of harp. There are also orchestras that perform Western-style music. The Japanese movie industry is centered in Tokyo, too. Japanese films are popular all over the world.

Kabuki theater

Geisha

Mount Fuji

Yesterday, we traveled about 60 miles west to Mount Fuji, Japan's highest peak. Rising 12,388 feet high, Mount Fuji is a dormant (inactive) volcano. The last time it erupted was in 1707.

Japan is located on the Ring of Fire. This is a fault line under the Pacific Ocean where earthquakes and volcanic eruptions are common. About 50 of the country's 150 volcanoes still erupt! And, there are more than 1,000 small earthquakes in Japan each year.

Mount Fuji's famous cone shape is so beautiful. The Japanese consider this mountain sacred. They call it Fuji-san. "San" is a term of respect that means "sir." Each summer, thousands of pilgrims climb to a small shrine at the top.

Mount Fuji

Mount Fuji

Kamakura

Today, we took a short train ride to Kamakura. About 800 years ago, the city became a headquarters for Japan's first shoguns. Shoguns were military leaders who ruled the country and were protected by samurai warriors. Samurai means "one who serves." Samurai were soldiers who lived simply, obeyed their leaders, and would kill themselves in battle rather than surrender. Two of Japan's martial arts come from samurai fighting methods. A type of unarmed combat, called judo, means "the way of gentleness." Kendo, "the way of the sword," comes from samurai sword practice exercises.

Silhouette of a Kendoka

Kamakura

12

Paper fortunes at shrine

Shingen-ka festival

Today, Kamakura is a favorite seaside resort for busy Tokyo residents and tourists who come to see its more than 80 ancient temples and shrines. We visited the colorful Hachimangu Shrine, which was built by Japan's first shogun, Yoritomo Minamoto. But the most spectacular sight was Kamakura's famous 700-year-old Daibutsu, or Great Buddha. This huge bronze statue is 37 feet high and weighs more than 120 tons!

Nara

We continued our travels south to Nara. The city was founded in 710, and was the first capital of Japan. Our tour guide said Nara is the birthplace of Japanese civilization. During this time, the Japanese learned a lot about government, the arts, architecture, and religion from China.

Today, Nara attracts many visitors like us. There are old wooden houses and traditional restaurants. Shops sell Nara crafts, such as handmade brushes and ink sticks for calligraphy, wooden dolls, and handwoven linen. At Todai-ji, a giant 1,200-year-old Great Buddha is housed in the largest wooden structure in the world! And in Nara Koen (park), we fed some of the thousand deer that roam free. They're considered messengers of the gods.

Deer in Nara Koen

Kofukuji Pagoda

Osaka

Osaka is so different from Nara! It is Japan's third-largest city, and an important commercial and industrial center. There are also many religious shrines and museums, such as the one in the grand, 400-year-old Osaka Castle.

Last night we saw a performance of bunraku, a kind of puppetry that was created in Osaka. The puppets wear fancy costumes and are almost as tall as I am! Each one is operated by a team of three black-robed puppeteers who study for many years. I still can't figure out how they got a puppet to eat with chopsticks!

Kites flown on Children's Day

Osaka Castle

Food and Agriculture

You won't believe what I had for breakfast this morning—soup! A traditional Japanese breakfast consists of soup, rice, and pickled vegetables. Many Japanese also eat cereal, toast, and coffee.

Rice is served at every meal. Japanese rice is sticky, which makes it easier to pick up with chopsticks! Our guide told us only about 15% of Japan's land is suitable for farming. Wherever possible, steep hillsides are terraced to grow rice. Other crops include fruit and vegetables, wheat, barley, and soybeans. Soybeans are used to make tofu, which is used in many Japanese dishes.

Sushi

Persimmons drying

Country fruit stand

Rice fields

Buckwheat noodles prepared Kyoto style

As you can imagine, Japan's surrounding waters provide much of its food. The Japanese catch and eat more fish and seafood (including seaweed!) than any other nation in the world. One popular dish is sushi. Bite-sized pieces of raw fish or seafood (like octopus or sea urchin) are wrapped in vinegar-flavored rice and seaweed. I tried it, but I still like the cooked stuff best. My favorites so far are tempura (tasty batter-fried fish or vegetables) and yakatori (shish-kebab). No matter what you eat in Japan, it comes with tea. Tea is Japan's national drink.

Takamatsu

Our next stop, Takamatsu, is on the island of Shikoku, the smallest and least populated of Japan's four main islands.

This morning we visited the Ritsurin Koen. The 400-year-old gardens took 100 years to plan, plant, and grow. There's a really cool teahouse that looks like it's floating on water! According to the guidebook, Japanese gardens are as much of an art form as painting. Plants, rocks, and water are placed to encourage a feeling of peace and harmony. And, though space is limited, the Japanese have found many ways to bring nature close to them. Some popular ones are Bonsai (the art of growing miniature trees in pots), and rock garden arrangements.

Tea pavillion in Ritsurin Koen

Bonsai

Kumamoto

Next we traveled to Kyushu, the southernmost of Japan's main islands and the second-most populated. There are lush green fields, lively cities, steamy hot springs, and strange volcanic formations.

Yesterday we visted 400-year-old Kumamoto-jo, one of Japan's great fortresses. It has concave (rounded) walls that made it difficult to climb. There are also openings from which stones were dropped on enemies.

Today, we visited nearby Mt. Aso, one of the world's most active volcanoes. You can go right up to the smoking rim and look in. (Scientists do monitor the volcano's activity, so it's pretty safe!)

Tunnel of Vermilion torii gates, Kumamoto-jo

Kumamoto mother and son in traditional dress

Miyajima

We took a ferry to Miyajima, a small island in Japan's Inland Sea. As we approached, we saw the island's famous giant red torii (arch) rising out of the sea. Our guide said the 53-foot-high arch is one of the tallest in Japan. Past the torii stands Itsukushima Jinja. That's the island's ancient shrine, built out over the sea on wooden stilts. It is dedicated to three goddesses who were the daughters of the Shinto god of the moon and sea. In the past, Miyajima was considered so sacred that ordinary people were not allowed to set foot on it. Even today, no one is allowed to be born or die on the island!

Guardian dog

Lantern and torii gate in ocean

Hiroshima

It was hard for us to imagine that a little over 50 years ago this bustling, modern city was nothing but ashes.

In 1945, the United States, trying to end World War II, launched the world's first atomic bomb attack on Hiroshima. More than 200,000 people were killed, either by the bomb itself or by the deadly effects of radiation.

We visited Peace Memorial Park. In it stands the Atomic Bomb Dome. Its blackened remains are a reminder of the bomb's terrible power.

We saw the statue of Sadako, a young girl who died of a radiation-caused illness. Sadako thought if she folded a thousand paper cranes (a symbol of long life), she would be cured. Sadly, she died after making her 954th crane. Every year, children send thousands of paper cranes in her memory and for all the children who died in Hiroshima.

The Atomic Bomb Dome

Religion

Everywhere you turn in Japan, there seems to be a shrine or temple. Our guide says that religion is an important part of Japanese life. Most people observe rituals and traditions from both the Shinto and Buddhist religions. A small number of Japanese are Christians.

Shinto is Japan's oldest religion. It is based on a deep respect for nature. It teaches that spirits (called kami) live in all natural things, like mountains, trees, and rivers. The name means "way of the spirits." Shinto shrines can be seen in fields and on mountains, towering over roads, and even perched on buildings in busy cities!

Shinto temple

Buddha, Kamakura, Daibutsu

Buddhist
monk, Asakusa

Shinto
priest

Buddhism is an ancient religion that began in India. Buddhism spread to Japan from China and Korea. It teaches that people should lead kind, unselfish lives. It also says that the soul is reborn many times on its way to becoming perfect.

Today we visited a jinja, or Shinto shrine. After our guide washed her hands and mouth, we passed under the torii. She rang a bell and clapped her hands to make sure the god was awake and listening. Then she made an offering of rice cakes and flowers. She wrote prayers on a small piece of paper, which she tied to a string next to the prayers of others.

Kyoto

We're spending a few days in Kyoto, one of Japan's largest cities. Modern Kyoto includes industrial, commercial, and educational centers. But most visitors come because of the city's grand history. Kyoto was the home of the Japanese emperors and the capital of Japan for more than 1,000 years.

The emperor's court was the center of art, crafts, and culture. There are grand palaces, graceful gardens, and more than 2,000 Buddhist temples and Shinto shrines. The entire ceiling at one temple was covered in gold! At another, it took 17 monks to ring Japan's largest bell!

Geisha dancers on stage

High above Kyoto

Eigamura movie village

Kamo River

Yesterday we visited Nijo Castle. It's where the ruling shoguns stayed when they visited. The nearly 400-year-old castle was grander than the nearby Imperial Palace. Our guide said the shoguns wanted to show the emperor who was really in charge. I wondered why the floors at such a fancy place squeaked. The guide explained that they were an "alarm-system" to warn the shoguns' guards of intruders!

Kyoto

With both Shinto and Buddhist traditions, it seems there's always a festival going on in Japan. There are festivals for children, ancestors, fishermen, travelers, deer, dolls, flowers, kites, stars—and even snow! Japanese festivals are called matsuri.

Kyoto has some of Japan's most spectacular festivals. The three biggest are the Aoi, Gion, and Jidai festivals. The 1,500-year-old springtime Aoi (Hollyhock) Festival celebrates the continuing prosperity of the city. The summer Gion Festival is Kyoto's most popular. It thanks the gods for their protection with a grand parade of more than two dozen giant floats. The fall Jidai Festival features more than 2,000 Kyotoites in costumes from the 8th through 19th centuries.

Jidai Festival

Festival time or not, Kyoto has the most famous food in Japan. For our last dinner here, we enjoyed the city's famous kaiseki ryori, an elegant full-course meal that was originally part of the tea ceremony. Plate after plate of the freshest, most beautifully arranged and delicious food came to our table. What a treat!

Kyoto chefs

Nishi-Koji market

Takayama

We traveled northeast from Kyoto to Takayama. This city is in the Japanese Alps, which are the north-south mountain ranges of Honshu's central region. Our tour took us past rushing rivers, forest-covered mountains, and snowy peaks. The 1998 Winter Olympics were held in nearby Nagano.

Walking in the old sections of Takayama (or taking a rickshaw ride!) is like stepping back in time. There are tiny tearooms, fine old homes, inns and temples, dye houses, and sake (rice wine) breweries. We saw Takayama's festival wagons, called yatai. These huge wooden wagons are nearly 200 years old. Many have puppets that perform tricks and amazing stunts!

Rickshaw

Temples in the snow

Wooden dragon float

Wood painting, Ten Shoji shrine

Today we visited the nearby Hida Folk Village, an open-air museum of traditional farm houses gathered from all over the region. Local craftspeople were demonstrating lacquering, wood carving, and weaving. The Takayama area has been famous for centuries for the beautiful work of its artists.

Hokkaido

Our train from Honshu to Hokkaido traveled through the Seikan Tunnel. That's the second-longest underwater train tunnel in the world! Hokkaido is the furthest-north and second-largest of Japan's four major islands.

We've been staying in Sapporo, the island's bustling capital. I was surprised to learn that the city was designed more than 100 years ago by an American architect!

Hokkaido was first settled by the Ainu, Japan's original people. There are only about 20,000 Ainu left. They speak their own language and have their own religion. They believe the salmon, bear, and killer whale are sacred.

Hokkaido

Children in Hokkaido

To many Japanese, Hokkaido is a wild, untamed wilderness. There are snow-covered mountains and bubbling hot springs. There are also thick forests and fields of wildflowers, sparkling lakes, and great marshlands. Bears, monkeys, and deer still roam. The beautiful red-crested crane, the Japanese symbol of long life, makes its home here.

Hokkaido's wide open spaces and cool, wet climate make it important for agriculture. Potatoes, corn, wheat, and beans are grown here. It is one of the few places in Japan with enough room to raise dairy cattle.

I wish we could come back in the winter for the Snow Festival in Sapporo. More than 300 enormous snow sculptures, from animals to famous buildings, are created. Some are as as tall as a ten-story building!

Glossary

Calligraphy the art of beautiful handwriting.

Emperor the male ruler of an empire.

Fault line a large crack in Earth's surface that can cause earthquakes.

Karaoke people sing the words to popular songs while a machine plays background music.

Legend a story handed down from earlier times.

Pilgrim someone who goes on a journey to worship at a holy place.

Prosperity success.

Radiation particles sent out by radioactive material.

Sacred holy, or highly respected.

Shrine a holy building; a place honored for its history.

For More Information

Books

Baines, John. *Japan* (Country Fact Files). Chatham, NJ: Raintree/Steck Vaughn, 1994.

Bunce, Vincent. *Japan* (Places and People). Danbury, CT: Franklin Watts, Inc., 1997.

Scoones, Simon. *A Family From Japan* (Families Around the World). Chatham, NJ: Raintree/Steck Vaughn, 1998.

Video

Japan (Travel Preview Series), 1995.

Web Site

Kids Web Japan

Learn more about the regions, sports, politics, climate, daily life, and economy of Japan. Ethnic traditions, recipes, and folk stories are also featured— www.jinjapan.org/kidsweb

Index